KU-568-999

and hold each other's hand.

Hello!

Best friends laugh and dance at parties...

My best friends

Written by Anna Nilsen
Illustrated by Emma Dodd

JN 03650684

LINCOLNSHIRE
COUNTY COUNCIL

Best friends smile and say hello,

...and play games like hide and seek.

Best friends give each other presents...

... and share their favourite toys.

Best friends put on grown-ups' shoes when they play at dressing up.

... **and swoosh and splash in paddling pools.**

Best friends take each
other home for tea,
and always share their
treats and sweets.

Best friends sometimes fall out and fight...

... but soon make
up and have a hug.

**Best friends get tired
and angry...**

Best friends tell each other secrets.